The Rainbow Bubble

by

Alicia Fadgen

With Illustrations by Emily Ann Evans

The Rainbow Bubble by Alicia Fadgen

Published by Pen It! Publications, LLC in the U.S.A.
812-371-4128   www.penitpublications.com

ISBN: 978-1-952894-71-8

Illustrated by Emily Ann Evans

This Book Belongs To:

_____

"Mom! There is a rainbow! I'll be back."

Johnny Patrick slammed the door and raced through his yard toward the woods.

He is on a mission. A mission to find the end of the rainbow.

From a very young age, Johnny loved all the things about St. Patrick's Day. Mainly because his family is proud to be Irish.

His middle name is Patrick.

His favorite color is green.

He is always on the lookout for a
four-leaf clover.

He loves hearing stories about
the Leprechaun.

He even loves when it storms.
Because sometimes after a storm,
came a rainbow.

He always wanted to find the end of the
rainbow where the pot of gold sat.

On this gloomy Saturday, he was touched with the Luck of the Irish.

A beautiful, bright rainbow soared through the sky.

Johnny quickly made his way through the woods, following the rainbow with his eyes.

"This is going to be it!"

He noticed something floating in
the distance.

"A bubble? Where did this come from?"

Johnny went to pop it, but instead it started to grow ginormous.

It grew bigger than his body
and the bubble snatched him up!

"Woooaaaahhhhhhh."

Johnny was now inside the bubble
and was being lifted into the sky!

His stomach moaned and his hands
became sweaty.

The bubble started to make its way toward
the rainbow.

POP!

The bubble suddenly burst!
Johnny slowly opened his eyes.
To his amazement, he was sitting
on the rainbow.

He was one step closer to the pot of gold.

Still in shock, he slowly walked along
the rainbow.

He saw something laying on the rainbow
a little further up.

It was a bird with a broken wing.

"Chirp, Chirp, we need help!" the bird said.

Another bird quickly swooped down.

"His wing is broken. I need you to get me a small stick and some weeds," Johnny said to the new bird.

The bird flew down into the woods and returned with the supplies.

Johnny placed the stick on the bird's wing and wrapped it with the weeds.

"This will keep you out of pain until it heals."

He had gained that knowledge from being in the Boy Scouts.

The bird gratefully flew away.

He continued down the rainbow.

A dark cloud slowly approached.

It hovered over Johnny and started to pour.

"Oh no! Go away! You are getting
me all wet!"

"I can't stop crying," the cloud sobbed.

"I know a good joke," Johnny said to the cloud, "Knock, Knock."

"Whose there?"

"Boo."

"Boo who?"

"Would you stop crying already!"

Just like that, the rain let up, and the cloud let out a thunderous laugh.

Johnny giggled and continued on.

He started sprinting down the rainbow
until...

SPLAT!

He landed on his face. He had tripped over
a crack in the rainbow.

"We need your help," a voice called from
below. It was the rainbow!

"Our colors have been mixed up. Can you
help us get them back in order?"

Johnny looked down at the colors. Confusion filled his head.

"Ms. Riley taught us a pretend name to help us remember the order of the colors in the rainbow. If only I could remember that name. Was it *Rog Y Vib*?"

"Okay. Get in this order Red, Orange, Green, Yellow, Violet, Indigo, Blue."

The colors got in order but the crack remained.

"Hmm. *Roy G Biv*? Red, Orange, Yellow, Green, Blue, Indigo, Violet."

"It worked!" The colors cheered.

Johnny was happy to help. And even more happy to see the end of the rainbow ahead.

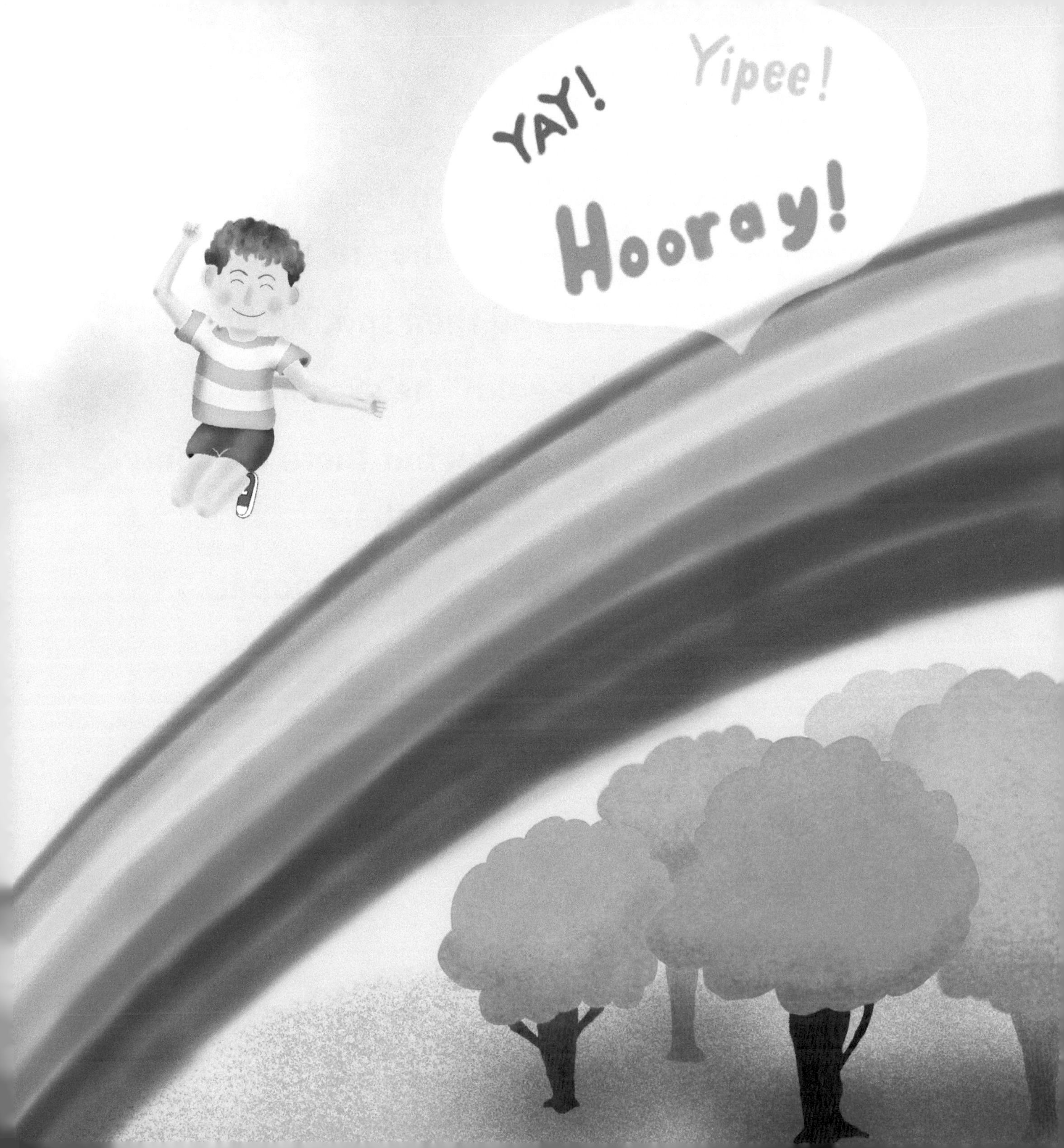
YAY!
Yipee!
Hooray!

Excitedly, he slid down the rainbow
and landed on the grass.

He looked around and then spotted the pot!

"Bring on the gold!" he exclaimed.

He peeked over the side, but there was only
a bubble sitting there.

Disappointed, he started to pop it.

It started to grow, and inside, it showed his journey down the rainbow.

It showed all the help he had offered others along the way. That was the true treasure.

Gold would have been fantastic, but looking out for others, was much more fulfilling.

Johnny smiled, "Bubble...I am ready to go home."

Johnny floated back into his yard. He sat down in the grass, and brushed through the clovers, hoping to find a four-leaf clover.

The End

CPSIA information can be obtained
at www.ICGtesting.com
Printed in the USA
BVHW021545230720
584441BV00002B/19